T0070215

4th book in the series:
The Five Stages of Love

WE PROMISED:
A Story of Abiding Love

by Linda Kay

authorHOUSE®

AuthorHouse™
1663 Liberty Drive
Bloomington, IN 47403
www.authorhouse.com
Phone: 1 (800) 839-8640

Published by AuthorHouse 09/07/2017

ISBN: 978-1-5462-0708-5 (sc)
ISBN: 978-1-5462-0707-8 (e)

Dedication

To all who face mental, emotional, and health challenges and to those who honor the marriage vows to love and cherish in sickness and health. Also to those brilliant minds continuing to invent or devise equipment to assist the physically challenged to enjoy life independently.

Contents

Cast of Characters

Colin - Husband (Papa)
Carrie - Wife (Nana)
Adele and George - Parents of Carrie
Margaret - sister to Carrie
Sandy - Friend to Carrie
Joyce and Keith - Parents of Colin
Jack - oldest brother of Colin
Lyle - brother of Colin
Ian - middle son
Shari - Daughter in law and wife of Ian
Marcie - Granddaughter, daughter of Ian
Megan - Granddaughter, daughter of Ian
Dean - oldest son
John - youngest son
Mary - Colin's sister
Jim - Mary's husband
Susie - Mary's daughter
Bertha - Farm owner
Amy and Ken - friends
Cal - Colin's hired man
Lexi - housekeeper
Bailey - Dog #1
Max - Dog #2

Prologue

"And now these three remain: faith, hope and love. But the greatest of these is love." 1 Corinthians 13:13 (NIV)

My name is Mary. In my observation, many marriages last a short time and succumb to the challenges of everyday life. I have watched my brother Colin and his wife Carrie cope with these demands over the years. Recent events have tested the bonds of their marriage. On several visits to the farm where I grew up and where Colin still farms, they shared their story, truly an inspiration that I now share with you.

***

Carrie Carlson sank into her lift-chair recliner in the family room, raising the footrest with the hand controls. Decor on the walls of the room reflected a country theme. Furniture spoke warmth and comfort with two antique pieces from family placed along the far wall. Her two granddaughters spent the day with us. Her parents would arrive later to share a family dinner. She looked tired, and raising her feet would help with the swelling. I joined them

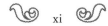

with my teacup in hand, enjoying their enthusiasm. They are beautiful girls of ten and seven, full of energy, long blonde hair falling around their shoulders. Marcie and Megan adore their grandmother, and she them. Marcie plopped down on the end of the couch next to her chair.

"Nana, tell me how you and Papa met," Marcie said quizzically, propping her chin on her hand with elbows on the armrest.

"I think I've told you this before, haven't I?" Carrie smiled at her, knowing the answer to her question, reaching for and patting Marcie's small hand.

"Maybe part of it. But Megan hasn't heard the story." Megan sat on the floor nearby, munching on a fresh cookie from the oven.

For a silent moment, I wondered if Carrie thought briefly about her life with her husband and family. If only things could be different. The years took turns she and Colin never imagined. Images of the two of them in their school days, filled with hopes for the future, danced in her thoughts.

***

Fall, 1968

"Carrie, you are only in the seventh grade, and too young to go on a date." Carrie's mother was explicit, and she was not excited about letting Carrie meet up with a boy. Carrie was petite and blonde, her hair cut short and curled with a perm. Adele James watched her blue eyes and sweet, round

face as she pleaded her case, her cheeks flushed with excitement.

"Mom, I'm almost thirteen, and we are just going to the movie. We'll be with lots of friends. Pleeeease? His brother is going to bring him into town. We'll go straight to Sandy's after a soda."

"Not quite thirteen yet, I might emphasize. Wai 'til your dad gets home, and we'll see what he says. I know Colin is a nice boy, and we know his parents." Adele bustled about in the kitchen, preparing dinner. George was due home any minute. "Where's Margaret?"

"I don't know. She got into a car with somebody after school, and I rode the bus home."

Adele wiped her hands on her apron and grasped Carrie's shoulders. "We will talk about this with your dad after supper. Now go do your homework." She released her daughter and used hot pads to check on the roast in the oven.

Colin Carlson was finishing eighth grade and going into high school. Also blonde and blue-eyed, Colin had an air of confidence and was popular in his class. He lived five miles out of town on a farm, so he could not be in town very often to hang out with friends. His brother, Lyle, would drop him off in town for various activities to meet up with his friends. Lyle was a junior at the high school.

The dinner table was quiet with little conversation. Carrie knew Margaret would be in trouble when she got home. She was late for supper. It would not be the best time to bring up her

proposed meeting with Colin. She finished her meal and took plates to the sink to begin washing them, her heart heavy, and anger at Margaret rising in her throat.

"Carrie, come sit down for a minute. George, Carrie wants to meet her friend Sandy and Colin Carlson in town at the movie theater on Friday night. They will be with a bunch of other friends, and plan to go to Olsen's for a cola afterwards. She wants to spend the night with Sandy. What do you say?" Adele presented the information in simple terms.

George looked up at Carrie and took a sip of his coffee. "I know the Carlson kid, and he seems okay. Helped with hay baling last summer. You can go, but don't expect to be making this a regular thing! And you sit with your girlfriends. Straight to Sandy's after the soda. Now go do the dishes." George leaned against the back of his chair and lit a cigarette. His clothes were dusty from the fields. He never showered until after he had eaten and finished his work on the farm. "I've got a shipment of soybeans due in tomorrow. Gotta get the shed swept out yet tonight. Looks like a sunny spring day tomorrow."

Carrie hugged him. "Thanks, Dad! You're the best!"

***

So began the love story between Carrie at twelve and a half and Colin at almost fourteen, a story that would span

decades of happy times and challenges in farm country surrounding a small Midwestern town. *"When two children in school say they love each other, it doesn't mean very much to them, and they take it at face value. However, if those two children were to grow up and marry, the word love would have much more depth and meaning because the two would more fully comprehend what they were saying" (Angelfire.com).* The Greek verb form 'meno' translates as "intensive". *"'Hupomeno' means to remain in a place instead of leaving it; to stay behind or persevere." (Angelfire.com).* The Greek 'meno' is the word for abide. Pastor Bobby once preached about abiding love, using boards and a bolt, as you see on the front cover, to demonstrate the commitment. If the two parts are not firmly joined with a nut and a washer, the bolt will fall out or roll away, and the boards separate. Carrie and Colin are the epitome of abiding love.

Chapter 1

Carrie-Fall, 1968

I remember communication among middle school students was often a note handed from one person to another, or contacting a friend who knew a friend to pass along information. Such was the case for Carrie. I smiled as her granddaughter Megan climbed onto her lap, her legs stretched out on the footrest.

Carrie began the story Megan requested. "I lived with my parents, Adele and George, just a mile north of town on the farm. An old two-story house stood a ways back from the road, torn down years ago, with a barn and machine shed in the farmyard where these are to this day. I shared a bedroom with my older sister, Margaret. We tolerated each other, but did not get along too well. My older brother, Tommy, died from a bicycle/car accident when he was very young. It was a tragedy for the whole town at the time. My dad never got over it. He always felt there was something he might have done to prevent it. Both of my parents were from well-known families in the area, where there are still lots of aunts, uncles, and cousins."

"My dad raised corn and soybeans and had some cattle, and he was in a partnership with my Uncle Lou. He had so many good friends in town, as he always had a funny story to tell them over coffee at the restaurant. We didn't see much of your Grandpa George, as he was either working or bowling. He and Grandma Adele enjoyed being out with friends at parties and dances, so Aunt Margaret and me were home alone a lot. Mom worked part time at a little dress shop in town, so she bought some pretty clothes for me to wear. Margaret was never interested in girly, pretty things. Do you still remember Grandpa George?"

"I remember him!" said Marcie. "We used to visit him in the hospital. And I remember that old house, too. What was the house like, Nana?"

"Our bedroom was small with room for just one double bed, a dresser, and a chair. We had some posters hanging on the walls of Elvis and the Beatles. Margaret and I agreed on the Beatles, and we had a transistor radio that ran on batteries to play local music stations. We also had a record player that played both single records and albums. Our television was in the living room downstairs, so you can be sure we were watching when the Beatles made their appearance on the Ed Sullivan Show. That was a big deal for us at the time."

"Who were the Beatles?" questioned Megan.

Carrie laughed. "They were a group of four guys from England who sang great songs. I'll play some of their music later."

"I've seen pictures of that Elvis guy," said Marcie.

Carrie continued her story. "When I was in junior high, I started working hard to lose weight, as I always thought

being a little heavy probably kept me from making the cheerleading squad. Although one of the teachers who had her favorites said it because I was boy crazy. My grades were good, and I liked to play softball. We just played during our PE classes at school."

"My friend Sandy told me Papa Colin's friend said he liked me. Your Papa was in the eighth grade and everyone liked him. When I saw him in the hall, he smiled at me, and it made me blush. One day after lunch, we walked around the high school track together. He was so easy to talk to. I was always nervous about how I looked and what the other girls were saying about us. One day as we were all walking around the track outside at lunch time, Papa asked if I could go to the movie theater on Friday night. We used to have a theater right here in town on Main Street. He had a brother, your Uncle Lyle, who could bring him into town for the movie, but I told him I doubted whether my parents would allow me to go, especially if I was meeting a boy there. After lunch and before science class, I asked my girlfriend Sandy if she could go to the movie. She lived in town, and if she could go, my folks might let me. Sandy agreed. She asked if I could spend the night."

"That would be your first date?"

"Yes, I guess that's right. I don't remember what the movie was about. Papa sat behind me. He and his friends were laughing and having a good time. He bought me a soda and popcorn at intermission. After the movie, we walked to Olsen's. It was a little restaurant across from the theater. He held my hand. There were eight of us crowded into a booth, laughing and talking about the movie, and Papa sat next to me. At around nine o'clock, Sandy and I

3

walked to her house, and Papa left with his brother to go home. The next Monday, he gave me a note, telling me he really liked me. I was so excited. We saw each other over that next summer at the swimming pool and the theater, into my eighth grade year, when he was a freshman. He was kind of jealous and a little possessive."

"In eighth grade, Papa Colin told me he was going out with Lyle's girlfriend's sister, Janie, who was in my class in school. His brother arranged it for a double date. Over that summer and into the next school year, he did not contact me again. We had officially 'broken up'."

"Oh, no!" exclaimed Megan. "So how did you get back together?"

Carrie chuckled, tipping back her head and looking up to the ceiling. "Around Carnival time of my freshman year, I saw Papa in the hallway at the high school. I had just made the cheerleading squad and he was playing on the junior varsity team as a sophomore. He said he was no longer seeing Janie or anyone else, and wondered if I could go to the Carnival dance with him. I did want to see him again, so I agreed to meet him at the dance."

"Papa!" the girls called out. "Come and sit with us. Nana is telling us her story about the two of you, so we need to hear your story, too." My brother Colin had just come in from outside. He had a presence that radiated love and caring.

"Give me a chance to clean up and eat some supper, and it will be my turn." He hugged the girls and kissed Carrie before heading for the shower, his clothes covered with dirt from who knew how many sources.

Megan jumped down from the chair as Carrie lowered

the footrest, pulled her walker into place, and made her way across the family room to the kitchen. I joined them to lend a helping hand. Each of the girls got an assignment to prepare the table. The girls' parents, son Ian and his wife Shari, arrived, and we all gathered around the table for some of Carrie's lasagna, prepared with the help of the girls. Then it was Colin's turn at story telling.

Chapter 2

Colin-The Home Place

Colin brought some old aerial pictures of the farm to the kitchen table. "The wakeup call from my dad, Keith Carlson, echoed up the stairwell every school day, but on Saturdays, I might get to catch another half hour of sleep. Saturday morning was always a big breakfast day with bacon, eggs, gravy, and raisin toast. My mom, Joyce, worked about twenty miles away in a hospital, where she had started working when my oldest brother Jack started college. Jack had gone on to study for the ministry, and he and his wife accepted an assignment to a small congregation on the other side of the state. Brother Lyle was just four years older, and just three years ahead in school. Mary was married with three kids, and lived in town. There were thirteen years between Jack and me, ten years between Mary and me."

I laughed and mentioned, "Colin was supposed to be a girl, so I would have a sister."

Colin frowned at my comment. "That two-section stairway leads to the upstairs of this old farmhouse, but there were once four bedrooms. There was no upstairs bathroom, so all four kids and my folks shared the only bathroom downstairs in the house. The old coal-burning furnace left those rooms very cold in winter. Dad converted the furnace to propane with new ductwork bringing heat to the bedrooms. Each upstairs room had a different view. To the south and across the road, the Stein farm boasted prize Shorthorn cattle munching on scattered corn stalks. At the top of the slight incline began another neighbor's property, the house barely visible. Many of the farmers worked together on projects."

In my mind, I could visualize all that he described. Colin pointed to the photograph. "To the west, a long stretch of the family farm reached to the distant hedgerow. Corn stood in the first field, then the soybeans the rest of the way to the hedgerow. The first field used to be pasture, so the soil was rich and the yields were usually high during harvest. The land was flat, with only slightly rolling ground. Snowstorms used to cover the hedgerow, and we could climb up and over the hedge when the drifts crusted over."

"Wow! That's a lot of snow, Papa," chimed in Megan.

"To the east, a few fruit trees lined the garden area, and the old windmill still turns lazily in the breeze. The pump and water pipes removed, the structure still stands there and serves no real purpose. The first tree is cherry, often loaded with fruit in the summer. The second and third trees are apples, one golden delicious, and the other red delicious. Family and neighbors love picking apples from those trees. Sometimes the yield was so heavy; we had to set up a prop to keep the limbs from touching the ground. A pasture for a small herd of Black Angus cattle filled in the area from the garden to the property line and north to the old red barn, now planted in corn or soybeans."

"Finally, looking north, the outbuildings, most of which have been altered, stood in the farmyard. To the right, the old red barn accommodated the top of the corn sheller my dad operated for hire. He had to cut out a piece beside the door for it to fit. It also had the drop down door for the haymow. Some of the other doors had begun to sag with age and the effects of many years of weather changes. The chicken house stood between the shed and the corncrib. A large drive-through area between the two storage sections for ear corn allowed harvesting equipment to unload and pass through. Next to the corncrib, a small brooder house protected small chicks delivered in the spring. The machine shed housed a small shop area for tools as well as space for most equipment used for planting and harvesting. A gas tank stood at the corner of the machine shed for dispensing gas into the ever-thirsty tanks on tractors and trucks. A gas deliveryman drove up in his tanker truck to replenish the supply. Beyond the farmyard, more acreage spread out for corn and soybeans, some oats, and alfalfa."

Colin began to draw a sketch on a piece of paper. "The total farm is two hundred acres of prime growing soil. One woman, Bertha, purchased the property during the Great Depression in the 1920s for one hundred dollars an acre. My grandpa was the first to sharecrop with Bertha. She paid the real estate tax and any general maintenance; he furnished the equipment, and the rest they split down the middle, income and expenses divided between them. Eventually, with my grandpa retiring, Dad took over the farm. His folks moved into a little house in a small town north of here, where they lived out their lives. Grandpa used to come out to help with the farm almost every day, driving his old '46 Chevy. By this time, Bertha had become like a member of the family. During the winter months, Bertha went to her home in Florida. When she was in town, she came to family dinners and celebrations."

"Dad, I barely remember her myself. Wasn't she a really tiny lady?" asked Ian, smiling at his dad.

"She was little but mighty!" Colin leaned back in his chair and grinned. "I remember going to her house and playing cards. She loved playing cards, Kings on a Corner usually."

"But you are here on the farm now, right Papa?" asked Megan.

"I have always loved the farm. Close to my dad, I enjoyed work, especially in the fields, planting and harvesting. Also like Dad, I enjoy good food. A good breakfast with a huge glass of milk would fuel my body at least until lunch." More sketching took place as he talked, the girls peering over his shoulder.

"The kitchen cooking area in the old farmhouse was a small, long space, beginning with what was once a pantry, and ending with a closed in back porch, the original kitchen converted to a dining room. Next to the dining room was a large living room with a high ceiling. My dad put a dropped ceiling in there at one time. The master bedroom was in the southwest corner with a television/office room in the southeast corner. Dad built a closet in the bedroom when they lived here. We often had to share bath water, as the well water was limited. In a large open space in the basement, a showerhead sprayed out over a drain in the floor with no

9

privacy. Many times users of the shower streaked up the stairs from the basement, across the dining room, to their bedrooms to dress." Colin laughed as the girls covered their eyes.

"There were two times I was in serious trouble on the farm. The first was when I was just about four years old. I always loved to watch my dad do the milking in the barn. There was a little step from the barn into the cattle lot, and I sat there waiting for him to squeeze milk from the cow to spray my face. Suddenly one of the cows broke loose from her station and charged to the door. She knocked me over into the mud and grazed my side with her foot. I've been told that my dad was white as a sheet as he carried me to the house. My only injury was a scrape on my side from the cow's hoof."

I nodded, remembering that vision perfectly.

"It's a wonder you weren't crushed by the cow!" chimed in Marcie. Colin laughed and continued with yet another story.

"The second big event happened in the summer before kindergarten. I was riding my bicycle down the lane and didn't see a bulk milk truck coming on the road. I ran into the side of the truck and landed between the wheels. Dad and Jack came running, placed me on a board and got me out of the road and to the hospital. I had a broken arm and some bruises, and started my first year of school with a cast on my arm." Colin wrapped a dish towel around his arm and pretended to be injured. "They tell me when I came out of the anesthesia, I asked for mouthwash!"

"Ew! That's really scary, Papa," said Megan. "So tell us about being with Nana."

"Nana had my attention one day in elementary school. She was in just fifth grade and I was in sixth. I was walking by her classroom when I saw a friend of mine playing the game of jacks with a cute blonde girl I had never noticed before, but I'd never forget her from that moment on. She was beating him so badly he didn't even notice me standing next to him. He focused on watching how she could snatch up so many of the jacks and still grab the ball before it hit the floor, and I just laughed. You'll have to have Nana show you how to play jacks, if we still have some around."

"I don't know if I even remember how to play!" exclaimed Carrie. "And I'm definitely not quick with these hands anymore." Carrie was no longer able to make a fist with either hand.

"Two years went by and Nana caught my eye again. This time, I asked her if she could go to the movie on a Friday night at a theater in town. A friend and I sat behind these two cute girls, one brunette and one blonde. I can't remember what the movie was, because the girls were more interesting than the movie, and a friendly popcorn fight had more action. My friend turned his attention to the brunette, but I was focused on Nana. I couldn't see enough of her. During the summer, I would ride my bike five miles to town to see her at the swimming pool or at the city park. It was puppy love, but I knew Nana was special. This continued into my first year of high school, when I was a dummy and went out with another girl. We broke up for a long while."

"You were bad, Papa," said Megan. "Nana told us about that other girl!"

"We were both 'free' at the time the School Carnival Dance was coming up. I was a sophomore and Nana was

11

a freshman. I saw her in the school hallway one day, and asked her if I could have a dance with her at the dance. She thought I asked her for a date to the dance, because she met me at the door, danced the first dance and every dance after that. We have been together ever since. We could only see each other at ballgames, at school, or at the movies, or maybe at the swimming pool in the summer. I would be getting my driver's license the next summer, so we were excited that we would be able to go on a real date."

Colin rose from the table. "Nana, why don't you tell them about high school? I have a few phone calls to make to line up help for bailing hay tomorrow."

Chapter 3

Carrie Continues

O n one visit to town, I saw that the old high school building where Carrie and Colin renewed their romance no longer stood in its old spot. A new school is now just in front of where the old structure stood. Originally, the high school building stood just north of the grade school and it connected to the grade school with a hallway and some wide steps that led to the main floor. Every freshman was very excited to climb those stairs and finally be in high school. Above all the lockers lining the hallways were pictures of former graduates. Both Carrie's and Colin's dads graduated from the old high school in the '30s.

Carrie gave Marcie a quick hug. "As I told you, when I was in junior high, I had always wanted to be a cheerleader. By the time I was in high school, I was determined to make the cheerleading squad. My grades were better and I had slimmed down, so I thought I might have a chance. There were a number of girls trying out. We practiced together and we all competed in teams before the high school assembly. I was so nervous. All the students got a ballot

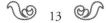

to vote on the top five girls for the cheerleading squad. The next day I found out, I made it. It was a very happy day for me, and I cheered every year after that. I worked hard at cheering both on the floor and on the sidelines. A newspaper photographer took a picture of me at one of the games, and I looked like I had been working out, my hair all matted down."

"I love to watch the cheerleaders," said Marcie. "I can try out for cheerleading in a couple of years."

"I was a cheerleader," said Shari. "Now I get to coach cheerleaders in high school, and that is so much fun. Some of them have a tough time with the acrobatics that are now required for competition."

Carrie laughed at a memory. "I remember showing your cousin Susie how to do the splits when I was babysitting with her for Aunt Mary. Sitting on the floor with your legs out, you just lean forward to touch your nose to the floor. You won't be able to do it at first, but if you keep working at it, spreading your legs out farther each time, you will eventually be able to bend all the way down to touch your nose. Susie was finally able to do these splits, and she was a cheerleader all through junior high and high school."

Both girls sat on the floor and everyone laughed as they tried to spread out and touch noses to the floor. "Nana, are you sure? I don't think my legs will stretch that far!" Megan exclaimed as she attempted the splits.

"Just keep trying, and you'll do it. The next weeks we practiced before the first basketball games. Papa was busy also practicing with the team. Whenever we had away games, Papa and I could sit together on the bus going to

the game and coming back. Sometimes we would get to go to a movie in town."

"A tradition at the high school still in place today is the all-school carnival. Each class elected a king and queen candidate, voted on by collecting money in jars at the businesses and by individuals carrying them around for donations. The competition at this event is fierce to this day. All money earned by the class went toward senior trips."

"When I was a sophomore and Papa was a junior, we represented our classes as candidates. Between us, we had many friends and relatives to help with the donations, and each of our classes supported us. In addition to being candidates, we all worked hard on the carnival, setting up games and booths and serving refreshments, planning our skit for the final night of the carnival. I don't remember what our skit was about, or Papa's class either, but at the end of the skits, we were crowned the king and queen of the carnival. Here's a picture of the two of us." Carrie opened an album with the picture.

"Wow, Nana! You were so pretty, and Papa looks so handsome with that long hair! Do you still have your crown?" Marcie and Megan were full of questions, but looked to her to continue the story. The picture of the two of them gave the girls a new perspective of their grandparents.

"No, I don't have my crown or Papa's. they belonged to the school for each new king and queen every year."

"What did you do when you weren't cheering or going to school?" asked Marcie.

"Papa had his driver's license, and we could go on dates. I babysat with Aunt Mary's kids. Her oldest daughter, Susie, was so bossy, but we got along fine, and she is a good friend

now. My mom and dad continued to spend lots of time away from home. Margaret got out of school later that year, and she got married. I was home many times by myself, if I wasn't with Papa or babysitting. During the summer I played softball, and enjoyed being with my teammates. My cousins and I had some fun together, and I had close girlfriends in high school to do things with. Papa was often busy on the farm, helping his dad." Carrie flipped through the photo album to show pictures of friends and cousins, identifying them as they turned the pages.

"Because I was a cheerleader, I had to keep up my grades, so I studied very hard. I liked bookkeeping, but never thought much about going to college. Back in the '70s most of the girls in my class went on to find a job or got married. During my high school graduation ceremony, the guidance counselor announced a winner in a new category called the "I Dare You" award. The idea was to recognize a student who worked hard to achieve. And the counselor announced my name. I had no idea. My hard work really paid off. I walked up the aisle to accept the award, and everyone was clapping for me."

"Yea, Nana!" the girls exclaimed.

"Okay, where are we in the story now?" Colin returned to the living room, watching the pictures in the album as Carrie turned the pages.

"It's the king!" exclaimed Megan, as she bowed to her grandfather. They all laughed at her antics.

"Mom, this is so much fun. I don't think I've ever heard these stories before now!" said son Ian. "Dad, we only have another hour or so, but tell us what you remember about high school and your relationship with Mom."

Chapter 4

Graduation and Off to College - Colin's Story

Colin flipped through a few more pages in the picture album and leaned back in his chair. Carrie's memories of cheerleading and high school stirred more memories for him. His son Ian and his wife Shari, along with their two granddaughters and me, waited in anticipation.

"Something you may not know about me is that I played in the band. I played the French horn and trumpet in high school. We didn't have a football team, but we did have a band to march in parades around the area. We had to practice out on the track infield, and wear our scratchy uniforms. Otherwise, our band played at other school events like basketball games and assemblies." Colin smiled at the memory.

"Papa, we know you can sing!" chimed in Marcie, as Colin continued.

"I've been blessed with that ability, as have all others in my family. Now you are singing in plays as well, Marcie.

Some of my friends and I had a band and played at a few events. I was the singer for the band. But the most fun of all was being in the high school plays. I played the part of Lt. Joe Cable in *South Pacific*. He was an officer in the Marine Corp." Colin began singing, "There is nothing like a dame..."

"Papa, you don't need to sing that now!" said Megan, rolling her eyes.

"The most fun was in the *Music Man*, when I played the part of Professor Harold Hill. Our cast marched down through the audience singing. Can you march with me?" Colin got up and started singing "76 trombones led the big parade . . ." as he, strutting with Carrie's cane as a baton, started marching. I smiled at the memory of the play. The girls marched with him through the kitchen, through the playroom and bedroom, and back into the family room. They were giggling behind him. He sat down, the girls falling into him, to continue.

"I wish I could have seen you do that, Papa!" exclaimed Marcie.

He hugged her. "Music has always been a special part of my life, singing at weddings, funerals, church events, and in the choir. My first choir was at the church I went to with my parents, the Junior Choir in grade school, and then I advanced to the Senior Choir when I was in high school. You girls can carry on the tradition, as Marcie has already sung at your church. We always attended church in another town, not where I was in school. I had friends in both places because of the Luther League at the church. Luther League was a special high school church group you could attend after confirmation in eighth grade."

"Our brother, Jack, completed his studies to be a minister in the Lutheran Church. He attended college in Iowa, and then went on to seminary. I had visited him at the college with my folks, but with thirteen years between us, we didn't know each other very well. Knowing Jack's experience, and our parents' endorsement, I imagined myself at the college there as well."

"My ambition in high school was to study to be a doctor. I worked hard to keep my grades up so I'd be able to get into that study plan. I'm not sure why I wanted to be a doctor, but I decided to go to the college in Iowa, which would put quite a few miles between Nana and me. Nana still had one more year to finish high school. We decided to work it out, since I'd be home for holidays and in the summer time, and she might be able to go to Iowa for school events. So after graduation and the summer, I moved into a dorm in Iowa to begin my studies. It was hard being away from her. She kept on with her cheerleading and her studies, and I was engrossed in mine as well."

Colin's mind wandered to a conversation with Carrie before he left for school.

> *"Colin, I'm afraid you will find someone new and want to go out with someone else."*
>
> *"You know there is no one else for me, Carrie. Besides, you can come up to Iowa to visit sometime. I'm sure we can work that out. I'll call you every week."*
>
> *"You don't know yet who you might meet there. Will you just be honest with me?"*

> *"I promise. We will be in touch, and we will*
> *be busy with studies. This year apart will be good*
> *for us, so we know for sure we want always to be*
> *together. You have to trust me."*
> *"Okay. You know I love you."*
> *"Love you more."*
> *"No, love you more!"*

"What are you grinning at, Papa?" asked Megan.

"Oh, just something I remembered. In the summer after my first year, and after Nana's graduation from high school, I worked with my dad on the farm. Nana signed up to go to business school. One of my dad's neighbors told me one day he would let me farm his ground if I decided to come back to farm with my dad. It would be 160 acres of land, which made it seem like I might be able to make a living at farming."

Colin remembered how beautiful Carrie looked one summer day at the lake. They had worn swimsuits under their clothes in anticipation of a swim in the lake. He had saved up money to buy an engagement ring, and he shared with his parents his intent to ask Carrie to marry him. After a quick swim, they lay back on towels and a blanket in the grass. Colin put his arm around her and kissed her deeply. Then he reached into the pocket of his jeans to pull out a box.

> *"Carrie, I have spent a whole year away*
> *from you, and I want us to be together. Will you*
> *marry me?"*
> *"Yes, of course, I'll marry you. Do your*
> *parents know?"*

> *"I told them a couple of days ago, and they are happy for us. Just a little concerned that we are so young."*
>
> *"I'm sure my folks will be fine, but when shall we get married?*
>
> *"Let's go for next summer. I'll finish the next year at college in Iowa while you are working on your certificate. What do you say?"*
>
> *"Sounds like a great plan!" Carrie looked at the ring on her finger, stood up, and said, "Last one in the water is a rotten egg!"*

"Papa, you are doing that again, smiling to yourself!" said Shari, trying to imagine what he was thinking.

"Sorry. My parents had a building lot by a lake outside of town, where my brother Jack eventually built a home. One nice summer day, Nana and I went out there to go swimming and I asked Nana to marry me. She said 'yes'. This was the summer of '73. We would plan the wedding for the next summer."

"I wondered if that was what you were thinking of!" Shari exclaimed, nudging Ian.

Colin blushed and continued. "I returned to school in the fall in Iowa, and began to give more and more thought to farming and studying agriculture. After deciding to drop the medical program, my adviser at the college suggested I study social work, but that didn't interest me. I applied at the state college for the Agronomy program, and returned to Illinois to go to school there in January. Since Nana and I would be getting married in the summer, I lived at home

on the farm with my folks and drove back and forth to the city, usually three days a week."

"I knew you didn't graduate from the school in Iowa, but I didn't know all this about changing your major," said Ian.

"To help save money for the wedding and our new life together, I worked at a shoe store. My brother Lyle got me a job with the store where he was working. When people came into the store, I'd have to help them try on shoes. Some of them had very stinky feet!" Colin pinched his nose and made the girls laugh. "When I was at home, I'd help my dad with the farming, or work with a local contractor building houses."

"Nana, why don't you tell them about your days in high school after I left for college?"

Chapter 5

Carrie Left Behind

Carrie maneuvered her walker a little closer to the table, flipping through a few more pictures in an album. "It's so hard for me to remember all the details of those days. I know at the time it seemed like the days were so long without Papa there with me. He made it back here for my prom. Aunt Mary made my pink prom dress, and I still have it. I did get to go to see him at the college, which gave me something to look forward to. On this one occasion, there was a school dance at the college, so my cousin Amy and her boyfriend Ken and I drove to Iowa and went with him to that dance. It seemed strange to be going to a college celebration."

Megan looked at her with curiosity. "What did you wear to the dance?"

Carrie smiled, flashbacks returning to her at the question. "I wore the same dress from the prom here at the high school, and Papa bought me a corsage to wear on my wrist. There were so many people there, and Papa introduced us to his friends. Amy and I got ready for the dance at the dorm with the other girls, and Ken stayed in the boys' dorm. Papa and Ken picked Amy and me up in the girls' foyer. After the dance, we went out for pizza."

"Did you go there on the weekend, since you were still in high school?" asked Ian, pondering his mother's independence.

"Yes. Mom and Dad let me go, mostly because Ken and Amy were going. We drove to the college, which was about four hours away. I don't remember being nervous about the trip. I remember when your dad and I let you go with some friends to Florida one summer when you were still in high school." Everyone laughed as Ian grinned.

"During my senior year, I applied at the business school to be a medical assistant. Papa and I spent a lot of time together in the summer after my graduation, and, as he told you, he asked me to marry him. There was no question about my answer. We talked about how we might be together if he stayed at the school in Iowa after we were married. We didn't know if we would have to live in Iowa. At that time, he hadn't yet decided to come back to Illinois."

"How quickly everything changed for you before the wedding. I'll bet you were glad to be able to stay here in Illinois," said Shari.

"That's for sure. Mostly because I had no idea where I might work or where we would live."

"Seems funny to think of us being born and raised in Iowa instead of here." Ian had no idea there could have been a different life for him and his brothers.

"Speaking of work, did you go to work somewhere?" asked Marcie, standing close to her grandmother.

"After my graduation, I started working at the hospital,

and my job was to clean the bathrooms and the floors in the patients' rooms and the hallways. I remember asking if I could wear gloves because of the germs, and my boss didn't understand why I would need them, unless I had something wrong with me." Carrie smiled at that memory. "Things are a lot different now, with lots of concern for germs and the welfare of the patients. When I wanted to go part time because of school starting, I learned I would have to work weekends in the nursing home area of the hospital. That was hard for me, and not exactly a dream job. In the fall, I started classes at the business school. There were two semesters, the same as in college. Mom and I were also making plans for the wedding. My parents loved Papa, so they were happy for us."

I could see Marcie was trying to imagine Carrie as a student, working in a hospital. "Nana, did you have to wear a uniform?"

"We wore pants and tops they call 'scrubs' in the hospital, not our street clothes. I put them on when I got to work and left them there for laundry. I had some shoes I left in a locker there to wear as well."

"Did you have to drive into the city for school by yourself?" asked Ian, trying to imagine his mother as a college student.

"I had a friend from town who was a student at the school, and we picked up another girl in another small town to car pool. At that time, the school was not very expensive, and my folks paid for the cost. We rode together for the whole time we were going to classes. We had so much fun. They made the time fly by for me. The school was right downtown, so we got used to the traffic and parking in the

city. I remember bringing home lots of homework. There were medical terms and medical coding to remember for tests. We also had to do some lab time, so I learned to draw blood for testing, as well as to take blood pressures. There was also some accounting involved, because of the medical coding. One of the teachers was very strict, so I was kind of nervous around her."

"Ewww," said Marcie, looking up Carrie. "Did you have to stick a needle in people's arms?"

"I sure did. The school was for all different kinds of businesses. Once you knew what you wanted to study, in my case medical or dental assistant, your classes were specific to that certificate. One of my friends was studying typing and secretarial duties, and her studies were completely different from mine. In May, I earned a certificate in the medical and dental assistant program. While I was in school, Papa came back to live with his folks and drove to the city for college classes."

Marcie moved to sit on Ian's lap and leaned in toward her grandmother, her elbows on the table. "I want to hear about the wedding."

Carrie turned more pages in the album. "Early in the summer there was a huge bridal shower held for me at the church with so many people there. My mom started stacking all my gifts in the dining room of our house, until we could move them into an apartment. Then my cousins had a personal shower later, where I got lots of lingerie and pajamas. Our wedding was huge, with about 400 people invited, so we filled up the church. You can't imagine how many gifts we received, and these also went to the house and the dining room. I had a battle with bronchitis a few days before the wedding, and still had a fever the day of the wedding."

"There was never a more beautiful bride, despite her cold and red nose." Colin laughed, his arm around Carrie, and continued. "Our reception was held at the American Legion building, and we spent our first night at a hotel. Then we had a honeymoon week in the Ozarks."

"That's where we go to the lake house now!" chimed in Megan.

Carrie smiled, "We have always loved the lake and the area around it in Missouri. That's why we found the lake house!"

Colin looked on at one of the pictures from the album from the college years. "After the wedding we moved into an apartment in Bloomington, near the school where I would begin my junior year. We had about fifteen hundred dollars in our bank account, and our rent was only ninety dollars a month. I do remember our first grocery bill was forty-five dollars, and that was because we were stocking up. Tuition for me at that time was three hundred fifty-two dollars a semester. I drove a 1974 foreign car and Nana had a 1968 American car."

"I don't remember ever seeing a foreign car in your pictures!" exclaimed Ian, his brow furrowed. "Do you have a picture of it?"

"No, I don't think so," said Carrie, turning a few more pages of pictures. Then she reached for another album nearby. "Soon after the wedding, I started my job at an eye clinic in the accounting department. I loved the old posting machine we had in that area, and my medical coding training was important to my job. Papa worked at

the shoe store he told you about, part-time for that first year and in the winter of his senior year. I always thought it was so funny that he didn't want to wait on me when I came in to buy a pair of shoes. I guess he thought his manager would think he was just visiting with me."

"Girls, this is so much fun listening to Nana and Papa tell their stories, but we really do have to get you home to bed." Ian rose from his chair, smiling at the moans and groans from the girls. "Come on. Nana can tell us more stories later."

They gathered all their things together and walked out to the car with their grandpa. Carrie and I waved to them from the door, she with one hand on her walker.

Chapter 6

Colin and the Farm

C olin and I are very close. I live in Texas, but when family events call us back to Illinois, my husband Jim and I stay with Colin and Carrie on the farm, sharing memories from the past. Settling in from the drive up from St. Louis several months later, we sat in the dining room around the table. We all laughed at how curious their granddaughters were about the two of them on my last visit. With some prompting, Colin related more of their story, while Carrie brought out picture albums to share, carrying them in the special box on her walker Colin had made for her.

"Shortly after Carrie and I were married, Bertha signed over the farmhouse and the farmyard to Dad and Mom and us. I'm not sure of the exact time frame when Dad decided to leave the farm and turn the operation over to me, but it was probably around the spring of 1975."

"Were you expecting that?" I asked, tucking a pillow behind my back.

"Dad came up with it on his own. In fact, he hadn't even talked to Mom about it. Mom was still working at the

hospital in Lincoln. They were making plans with Jack to build the house on the lake. That summer I helped Jack with the house building, and when their house was completed, they moved in and we moved to the farmhouse. We agreed to buy the farm machinery and the appliances in the house over seven years, and to buy their half of the house from them. That fall Carrie was driving back and forth to the city, and I was working for a builder in town, while still studying in my senior year of school. We were bringing in enough money to begin our farming operation, although I'm not sure how we managed all of it. The farmer who had promised me the 160 acres to farm gave it to someone else, so I was very disappointed. I did pick up another 160 acres from another landowner. All of a sudden, we were fifty thousand in debt!"

"Yikes, that's a lot of money for a young couple to tackle," I said. Thinking back, I added, "And Carrie didn't work too long after you moved, did she?"

"We knew from the beginning we wanted a family, but decided we needed to wait a few years. That was until Carrie found out she was expecting. It was a dramatic change in our lives. She continued to work right up until the day she delivered Dean. We did attend some Lamaze classes to prepare and were very excited about the new baby. In '76, Dean was born. Carrie did not go back to her job at the eye clinic, but instead decided to be at home with the baby. Ian and John were born over the next several years.

"I remember those babies well!" I poured a cup of coffee, which Colin had set up in the coffee maker as he talked. Carrie joined us at the table to participate in the conversation.

"So, Colin, how did the farming go for you with Carrie at home with the kids? I can imagine it was a struggle."

Colin leaned back in his chair and rubbed his head, thinking. He continued, "Dad loved helping on the farm, so he was here many days. I kept finding things for him to do that he could manage. For a while, he worked at a welding shop in town and worked for the building contractor. I usually put him in the combine during harvest season, as it was the safest place. But he still worked hard and was the best hand a farmer could have. He marveled at the technology and was amazed at the yield monitor in the combine. I did pay him for helping, by the hour. I still remember the day when he couldn't get up on the John Deere 4020. That was it; he was done."

I thought about what he had said. "I remember how weak he got before his death. He was around to help on the farm for a long time. They were gone most of the winter to Florida, and it was good for him to get away from the cold. How did you get more acreage to farm?" I asked curiously, taking a sip from my coffee cup.

"Farming went pretty well for us through the late '70s and early '80s. I started cash rent leases in 1980, and others for whom I farmed also wanted to farm with cash rent. Most of these were on a sharecrop basis. Having to pay cash rent and shoulder all the costs for putting the crop in the ground was a big change. I also did some custom farming with other farmers in the area, including Carrie's dad and one of his neighbors. Later I took over some of the ground Carrie's dad farmed after his death. The most ground I farmed at one time was fourteen hundred acres."

"No wonder it took a long time to get all those crops

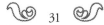

harvested!" Jim laughed. "Back in South Dakota, we had quite a bit of acreage, but didn't do any custom farming." I walked into the kitchen to get the coffee pot, and poured everyone another cup, grabbing a soda for Jim.

"In the winter months, we started remodeling some of the old farmhouse. Since I had picked up some skills working with Jack and others, I first tackled the high ceiling in what is now the family room. Dad put up a dropped ceiling, so the space above it was in disrepair. We repaired the plaster on the walls and ceilings. I'm not sure of the year, but another project was building the cabinet here in the dining room. Carrie was excited to see how it turned out, and I knew then I could do a lot more with wood. We used one of the bedrooms to convert to an upstairs bathroom. As the boys were growing up, we needed more space."

"Those bedrooms all look fabulous now, thanks to Carrie's decorating. The bathroom was a great addition for the family." I looked at the oak cabinet. "This china cabinet is beautiful, and I remember when you completed it. I was amazed! Were there particular years of tough times with the farm?"

"The drought hit us in '88. The hay business was the one thing that saved us. The government had initiated a "set aside" program the year before to help stabilize grain prices by controlling production. I had put my set-aside acres in oats and alfalfa the year prior and had a good stand established. Alfalfa has a deep root system and the crop made it through the drought. We started getting rain in August and it really took off. The government released the set aside acres for grazing and baling because of the

short feed supply. We baled everything we could. We even shipped hay to Texas and Missouri. Luckily, '88 was the first year I had taken out federal crop insurance. We had to borrow a substantial amount of money to put out the crops and didn't want to risk it all. In the end the insurance helped pay operating expenses, but we still had capital debt to pay."

"I remember when my dad struggled back in South Dakota during those times of drought. There were lakes so dried up I could walk across them, hunting pheasant. It was a very dark time for farming and a number of farmers went broke." Jim shook his head remembering those times, and looked to Colin to tell more. "What led up to that time here?"

"Farmers had been able to buy land in the '80s, as prices increased on acreage, and the banks loaned the money. Then when the drought happened and prices for crops tanked, many had to turn back their land and file bankruptcy. Carrie and I rarely argued, but when we disagreed, it seemed like it centered on money. She sometimes got angry with me if I wasn't spending enough time at home, but we always were able to work through our differences and tried to never go to bed angry with one another."

I smiled, patting Carrie's hand. "That's a good practice, but I can sympathize with Carrie."

"Financially we had a big shakeup shortly after the drought. Bertha called me and asked that I stop by her home in town. You remember by this time, she had lost both her sister and her niece who would have one day inherited her property. Bertha loved the boys, and she told me she wanted the farm to stay in our family. She then told me she had drawn up paperwork to give us the farm. I don't

even remember what I said, I was so flabbergasted. I drove home to share the news with Carrie. Of course, we felt very grateful and humbled by this news. The only challenge with the gift was the requirement for us to pay the real estate taxes for that year, and I now had to get the funds for the entire acreage to plant the next years' crop!"

I laughed, "Wealth on paper, poor in cash!" as Colin shook his head. "Carrie, we want to hear about raising the boys on the farm when we get back from an errand this afternoon. Why don't you plan to meet us in town for dinner . . . we'll buy!"

Chapter 7

Raising Three Sons on the Farm

Jim and I drove to a nearby town to visit some friends from our old neighborhood, and met Carrie and Colin for dinner before returning to the farm. We gathered in the living room and chatted about the day. Carrie returned to her recliner, standing up from her motorized chair and navigating with the help of her walker. I marvel at her determination.

I commented, "We lived out of town for much of the boys' growing up years, even though we all talked often by phone. So tell me about the boys."

Carrie smiled. "Colin is right about me being angry because he didn't spend enough time at home. From when the boys were little, our life was an endless run of trips to town for sports and school events. You remember your mother gave me the rocking chair at the time Dean was born. I had so much fun being home with him and spending some time with my mom."

"I'm sure your mom enjoyed that time as well, Carrie."
I tucked my feet under a blanket on the couch.

"We planted a huge garden, which kept me busy
planting, weeding, and then harvesting and canning or
freezing the produce. I had never done much of this before,
but your mom and my mom helped me when they could.
Then Colin also planted rows of sweet corn around the
field corn. The corn did so well we gave away as much as
we used. We stripped the corn from the cob and packed
it into the freezer, as we did with many other vegetables.
That old Hotpoint freezer your folks had lasted us for many
more years."

"That is really a dinosaur, for sure," I said. "I remember
it sitting in the corner of the dining room, kind of crowding
the table. Dad always got a huge ice cream tub from the
food delivery truck, and we had ice cream for nearly every
supper."

Carrie adjusted in her chair slightly and continued,
"Out on the farm, the boys could always find something to
get into. They built forts and tunnels in the hayloft. In the
winter, they would build igloos in the snow or make giant
snowmen or snow dogs. We built a snow dog one winter
that looked so much like a real dog that Bailey, our Golden
Retriever, started barking at it as if it was a threat. Bailey
was the most protective of the boys of any dog we had.
The boys built a fort out of concrete blocks one summer
out by the hedgerow. Not realizing one of the blocks was
home to a large nest of wasps, the boys found themselves
under attack. Bailey came to the rescue and started biting
them and chasing them off, taking the stings himself. The
boys never got stung, and they remember his heroic effort

that day. Bailey also kept a skunk away from Dean one time when he was playing in the barn. When the boys were outside, Bailey would go everywhere with them."

"He was really a beautiful dog."

I smiled at a flashing memory of Dean as a youngster. The family had gathered for Christmas, and my kids, being older, were reading the tags and handing out gifts.

"There's one more kid here, Dean!" Dean exclaimed, concerned.

"I was just remembering Christmas times with the family, when the boys were all little. My girls were always playing with them, playing school on the steps at Dad and Mom's house. Sometimes they would play games like Hide the Button. Please go on. I love hearing these stories."

"We built a playhouse one year above the well platform," Colin continued. "It was about six feet off the ground. John had his superman pajamas and cape on one day when Dean and Ian convinced him he really was superman and could fly. So John took a flying leap off the playhouse platform, only to find he couldn't believe his brothers anymore. They showed him how you could jump up and touch the electric fence and not get a shock. John couldn't get off the ground very far and always got zapped. As the boys got older, they were always close and never got into any big fights. We were very proud of them. Of course, we kept them busy on the farm and encouraged them to get involved in sports and school activities."

Carrie opened yet another album. "When I look back now, even though there were a few years between each of the boys, the time seemed to go by quickly. I enrolled the boys in dance classes to help with coordination. We still don't know how we managed to get them to all their

activities. Dean was into wrestling in sixth grade and Ian and John got into Boys Club Basketball. We enjoyed taking grandparents to as many games as we could all through high school. The boys were in school plays and musicals. Dean surprised us his senior year with the lead in *Li'l Abner*. He did a great job."

"Ian was a little more ornery and drove the play director crazy." Colin shook his head. "During one play practice she demanded all cast members be on the stage 'immediately or else'. Ian came out from behind the curtain wearing just a jock strap. We still hear stories when we have family get-togethers about some of their antics. John was the most musical and taught himself to play a guitar and saxophone. He was in a Christian rock band and had the lead in *South Pacific* and *Oklahoma* in high school."

"He has such a beautiful voice. I understand he still plays for his church in town." I stood up from my cozy spot. "I'm getting a glass of water. Can I get something for anyone?"

"I'm good, thanks, Mary. John and some friends have a group that sings Christian music at the church and at some other churches in the community." Carrie smiled, pleased at John's accomplishments.

"One of the most terrifying moments as a parent is when you hear that one of your children has been in an accident," continued Colin. "We had just arrived home from visiting Dean at college one Sunday afternoon. Ian was fifteen and nearing his sixteenth birthday. Dad had given him permission to use his car while they were in Florida for the winter, but not until he turned sixteen. Ian's job was to wash the car and get it cleaned up while we were gone. The message on the phone recorder told us Ian had been in an accident and was at St. Francis hospital. He took the car for a drive through the country roads and had a near head-on collision with the old car hanging over the edge on a bridge. We went directly to the hospital." Colin leaned back in his seat, reflecting on the event.

> *"Are you okay?" Colin and Carrie arrived at the emergency room.*
>
> *"They think my nose might be broken, and I have this cut," Ian replied, almost in tears.*
>
> *"What were you thinking, taking the car out for a drive?"*
>
> *"I stayed on the back roads. But Dad, it wasn't my fault. I was on my side of the road, and the other guy just came right at me!"*

"He just had a gash on his nose. Ian kept saying it wasn't his fault. The question was 'who was at fault?', since the police didn't issue a ticket. I went to the scene of the accident and took pictures of the skid marks and damage. The insurance company totaled Dad's car. It was pretty old at the time of the accident. At just about the time the statute of limitations was set to expire, we got a summons and were being sued for causing the accident. We got a lawyer and showed him the pictures of the accident scene. We believed Ian's story of how he saw the other driver lose control of his car as he approached the bridge, causing him to swerve and cause the collision. We went to court and won the case. The judge ruled that the other driver was at fault. Ian being under age didn't matter in this circumstance. Ian had to

 39

have surgery on his nose, and the court awarded him a nice settlement. It was a very tense time at our house!"

Jim rubbed his chin, considering the outcome. "So if you hadn't taken those pictures, you may have lost the case. Just goes to show you have to be your own advocate and anticipate possible outcomes. I hadn't heard that story before."

"Back to the farm," said Colin. "The boys were exposed to a variety of animals. We bought four bred gilts one year and converted a portion of the barn into a farrowing house. Each gilt had twelve pigs and the boys had to care for and feed them. They learned a lot but really didn't like the dirty work. We did this for two years, and they made good money as hog prices were high. We had a salmonella outbreak the second year and it could have wiped out the whole herd. We caught it in time and were able to vaccinate the pigs to bring them back to health. We raised chickens a couple of years, but the boys probably enjoyed raising cattle the most. Watching newborn calves grow, bucket feeding, and having the bull chase you across the pasture are some of the memories they share. One time a cow dropped her calf in the muddiest place on the farm. The cow had a mean disposition and wouldn't let me near it to help it out. We rolled a round bale feeder over the calf so we could safely get to it, and we had Dean back the four-wheel drive pickup to the feeder. I threw the calf to Ian in the back of the truck and hopped in. John opened the gate and Dean was able to drive out of the lot. John closed the gate before the cow could catch up. It was a real team effort. After we cleaned the calf, we returned it to its mama."

"Oh, my, that was quite an event! Any number of things

could have happened to you guys. I'll bet the boys were so excited!" We laughed at the image of the three of them trying to rescue the calf.

I stood up from the sofa and stretched. "It's been a long day. Jim, let's head up to bed, what do you say? We can hear more of these stories tomorrow. You cookin' breakfast, Colin?"

"We'll have biscuits and gravy at eight o'clock."

Chapter 8

Colin and More Changes

Colin was busy in the kitchen early the next morning preparing biscuits and gravy, the coffee brewing and the aroma rising up the stairs to our bedroom. Dressing and making our way to the kitchen and dining room, we enjoyed his cooking expertise. After some laughter over stories about the boys that Colin and Carrie shared the night before, I asked him to tell us more of their story.

"For years I had been banking in town, and the bank there was bought out by a larger bank in Missouri. One of the worst crises in my memory happened when this 'big' bank cut everyone's operating line of credit back 25 percent in 1991. We had a bad hay crop that year, which we depended on for our tax payment. I asked my loan officer if I could secure another twenty-five hundred dollars to pay my taxes. This was when everything had to go to the Missouri facility for approval, and they rejected my request. I was furious. I took all my loans to a farm-oriented bank in a nearby town. Afterwards I got a call from some VP at the Missouri bank wondering why I had left. After I blasted him with my situation, he checked into it and called me back. Evidently, there was a clerical error and the submitted request was for ten times the amount I had requested. He begged me to reconsider, but it was too late. I had to go to Mom and Dad to get the money to pay my taxes. The loan officer never apologized for the error. Dad taught me that things don't always go as planned, but everything always works out. Just have to have faith. That's why I don't worry, and it drives Carrie crazy!"

"If we heard that once, we heard it a thousand times when we were kids. If he was worried, we never saw it." I smiled at the memory of my dad, always positive.

"There came a turning point in our lives when we knew we had to do something if we were going to send our boys to college. Dean enrolled at a private college with a high tuition. There just wasn't going to be enough money. On my annual trip to the bank to secure financing for the next crop, my loan officer at the new banking facility asked me if my wife worked anywhere. I told him about the job she held at the eye clinic, and she had helped you, Mary, in your office during tax season. Carrie also kept all the books on the farm, drove tractors, combines, and lawnmowers while holding kids on her lap. She worked at home, but was away from the office for a long time."

"Why do you ask?"

"The bank is growing and outgrowing our employees. We need good, reliable people to grow with us here."

> *"I don't know if Carrie would be interested.*
> *She has been away from the job market for quite a*
> *while, raising our boys."*
>
> *"I'll just give you this application, and you*
> *can see what she thinks. If she is interested, bring*
> *it back and I'll put in a good word for her."*

I sat back in my chair. "Gosh, I had completely forgotten about Carrie working with me during tax season. Am I ever glad I'm no longer doing tax forms!"

Colin laughed. "I had to convince Carrie to fill out the application and give it a try. She agreed to give it two weeks and if she didn't like it, I couldn't be mad at her. She would learn all aspects of banking and started in the loan department to learn loan processing. She nearly gave up, but by the thirteenth day, she started to catch on. She could do it! It was kind of another 'I dare you' moment."

Carrie came in from her shower. "I was sure it wouldn't be a fit for me, but I lasted for nineteen years!"

"Everything worked out with your crises with the banking industry," I said. "The smaller, hometown banks work much better with the farming industry than those big conglomerates. I want to hear more from Carrie about her job there later. So how was the college situation for the boys resolved?"

"When the time came for Dean to start college, money was tight. Since Dean had set his sights on a private college, I promised him we would find a way to make it work. He would have to work outside the farm and take on his own student loan. Scholarships and financial aid helped the first year. Dean worked the summer after his first year with Jack

in Indiana and made a decent salary, living there with Jack. However, because of his earnings, Dean lost his financial aid. If it hadn't been for Carrie and some creative financing, Dean wouldn't have been able to continue there. By his third year, it was time for Ian to go to college, but he had chosen a state school. The tuition was much cheaper and with two of our boys in college at the same time, it made for a lot more financial aid. John went to a private college three years later and was able to help with a combination of scholarships, student loans, and working as a resident assistant you know, on campus to reduce his costs. Now they have all finished college and have good jobs. We are pretty proud of them."

"My nephews are the best," I added. "Hopefully, Jim and I will get to see the rest of them while we are here."

Chapter 9

Carrie Goes to Work

C arrie maneuvered her motorized chair closer to the table, and Colin got her a plate of food from the kitchen. The chair was a recent, new addition and much more effective than a walker for her.

"Thanks, Colin. When I started at the bank, I was only making six dollars an hour, but the bank offered an ESOP, short for employee stock ownership program. I had so many friends at the bank and rarely missed a day of work. Each year I received a raise in my pay, and some of them were substantial. The interesting part of this was in some years the amount paid into my ESOP was more than my annual salary. My job was stressful with deadlines and government changes on loan processing. I really just wanted to be able to be back home. Who knew I'd stay for nineteen years?"

"Tell me about some of your positions at the bank and the challenges with co-workers." I was curious about Carrie's experiences.

"I actually started working on December 6, 1993. I planned to start out part time but it became a full-time job.

Dean was starting college the following August and we needed extra income. I was scared to death when I went in for the interview, but I must have done okay, because they called a couple of days later and hired me. I worked in the servicing department in loans replacing a guy who died while he was on vacation. The job was idle for two months. I had been home raising our kids for eighteen years and farming, so the transition was overwhelming. I knew nothing about banking. Besides me, there were three loan officers, a supervisor, two loan processors, and a receptionist. We were in the old bank building. The first week was terrible. Everyone was helpful, but I was really struggling. I told Colin I would give it two weeks. If things didn't get better I was going to quit."

Colin patted her knee and smiled. "I knew she was tough and could make it."

"Sounds like you were way over your head, sort of a sink or swim situation!" I laughed.

"Since our department was small we were all very close and helped each other. The bank started growing, so we added two more loan processors and servicing. After about three years, I trained an employee for my job when I moved to loan processor. It was another scary moment, changing jobs, but I survived and enjoyed it more than servicing. As the bank acquired more banks and we continued to grow, our department moved to a remodeled building two doors away from the old bank building. Our job now required all of the loan processors to meet with customers, file paperwork and work one Saturday a month. We typed loans and trained employees of new bank acquisitions. The

 47

processors grew from the original three to a larger number as the bank expanded."

I enjoyed working with the senior staff and the loan department in Carrie's later years at the bank, so was somewhat familiar with the dynamics. "The growth of the bank was really phenomenal in the '90s. The president had the vision, while his wife held the reins on expenses. What was the atmosphere like?"

"I have to say the first ten years of my job at the bank were the most enjoyable, working with all the employees. The loan department had its own Christmas party every year. We went out to eat, did gift exchanges, and played games. After the last party, word got around the bank about our parties, and other departments started complaining. The bank put a stop to those department outings. One of the bank officers came to the last party we held and entertained us with funny stories about the bank history. We laughed so much."

"Too bad the parties had to stop. When people get along well outside the office, it makes for lots more comradery at work." I thought briefly of Carrie's work history. "So that was the first ten years. I'm guessing the next years weren't as good?"

"After about eleven years, my good friend and I were called over to the manager's office. He and one of our supervisors promoted us to Assistant Vice President. I was very excited, but also a little nervous. There would be extra meetings and work load involved. No extra pay, but the benefits were better and it increased my percentage contribution to the ESOP. We were also required to go to more bank-sponsored outside events."

"Exciting for you, but I do understand the extra commitment." I picked up Carrie's plate and carried it to the sink. "Did you have some good friends in your department? Or was it all business?"

"The first three years I was good friends with Tammy. We ate lunch together often, and Colin and I got together with her and her husband. She quit after about four years because of medical conditions. When we moved to the new building, Sandy and I became close. Several of us would go to lunch until lunchtime changed to a half hour. With the job change to processors, there were only the three of us left. We did loan preparation and worked hard. We started to bring in food at holidays, and appraisers brought in gifts of food and other items for Christmas until once again the bank stopped them. As the bank kept growing with more employees on the payroll, the atmosphere of the bank changed."

"I guess bigger isn't always better," I said, filling coffee cups. Colin opened a sugar packet for Carrie.

Carrie stirred the sugar into her coffee pensively. "The bank moved us to a branch in a nearby town. Everyone hated it. The branch was huge and the drive was farther. We had only a half hour for lunch and there were no restaurants close by. That's when I broke my ankle. I was the last one upstairs that day, but managed to get out to my car with my broken right ankle. I don't know how I did it, but I got home. After the ankle repair and four weeks off, Colin had to drive me to work and pick me up in a wheelchair. I wasn't able to manage the crutches. I found out later it was because of my condition and limitations on my strength. We were upstairs and it was so hard for me to get around. After two

years, our department moved back to the main bank in the old building."

I touched her hand. "I didn't realize you were already feeling the effects of the disease at that point. You have fought through this for a long time. You stayed for a while longer?"

"The last four years were the hardest for me. We got a new supervisor and she favored the people she hired. I got along okay with her, but it wasn't easy. The laws and regulations changed and home loans were a nightmare. The training was not effective. All of us had to learn as we worked through them. I was just getting good at these when I moved to commercial loans, only because of the workload. By the time I left, the bank managed thirty branches. There were only three when I started."

"That really is amazing." I shook my head, considering the effect of so much growth.

"My last day was December 31, 2012. The girls had a cake and flowers for me on the 27th. For three days, people came in to say goodbye. It was wonderful. Connie took pictures of everyone and gave me a photo album when I went back to visit two months later. The group held a potluck for me and gave me the stone that is out by the door that reads 'Friends make special memories'. I made a lot of wonderful friends and memories at the bank. It was hard to retire, but it was getting very difficult for me to do my work with my increased weakness. I am so thankful for the album, and I look at it often."

I stood and put my arm around Carrie's shoulders. "What a truly lovely thing to do for you."

"During my years of working and being super mom

to the boys, we lost all of our parents. Your dad died in 2001, and Mother died in 2003. We were all very close to both of them. Then soon after Mother died, my mom got her cancer diagnosis. Treatments didn't stop the disease. I took as much time away from work as I could to take her to appointments and care for her. Eventually volunteers came to the house during the day. I went to the house after work to help my dad with food and laundry, then home to do the same for Colin and me. During this time, I became very angry with my dad. He depended on everyone else to care for Mom, and wasn't there for her like I thought he should be. She died in 2004, just six months later."

"There were so many times Carrie came close to retiring, but she was really motivated to do her job." I noted a tear in the corner of Colin's eye.

"Meanwhile, the boys were busy at their jobs, and John was about to graduate from college."

Abruptly, Carrie used the controls of her chair to move to the living room. Will you excuse me? I need to get my feet up for a bit."

Chapter 10

Colin on Carrie's Challenge

Alarmed at how long Carrie physically struggled at work, I prodded Colin for more information. "We were away for most of the time when Carrie started having problems. Refresh my memory as to how her disease was discovered." I had usually kept up with Colin by phone, but one can only squeeze in so much on a phone call.

"Not long after John graduated from college in 2005, Carrie started having some difficulty going up and down steps. It was subtle at first. She worried about long flights of stairs and had to take one step at a time. She started complaining of pain in her knees. We attended a wedding in the city on an upper floor. An elevator took us up, but we decided to take the stairs down. Carrie's knees gave out about half way down the stairs, and she fell backwards. She was more embarrassed than hurt, but it was time to see a doctor."

"Backwards? I'm sure she was mortified." I sat back in my chair.

"I had a real problem with our general practitioner. I

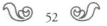

had an office visit with her when I was just about forty to renew my CDL license. She asked me about my sex life and told me about a little blue pill available if I needed it. Carrie really liked her and hated me calling her a quack. I don't think she did anything to help Carrie. This general doctor recommended an orthopedic surgeon. He determined a need for knee replacement surgery as the X-rays showed bone on bone in both knees."

Jim smiled at Colin. "Sounds like you had a lot of doctor visits to finally get some answers."

"I can't even tell you how many. Soon after the visit to the orthopedic doctor, Carrie fell at work. This time, she broke her ankle. She told me she didn't trip or stumble, she just fell down, because her knee gave out. After Carrie's fall at the bank, I went with her to ask our GP about whether some of the medications Carrie was using could be causing her muscle weakness. I can still see her with her little hammer testing Carrie's reflexes. She tried numerous times to get a reflex reaction in her knees to no avail. She took her off the cholesterol medication after I pointed out a possible cause of muscle deterioration. Just saying how you need to be your own advocate for your health and for your loved ones."

"I wonder if I need to check with my doctor about the cholesterol medicine I'm taking." I looked to Jim for a response and he nodded. Colin continued.

"This was now the fall of 2009. It was a long harvest that fall and we weren't able to finish until the first week in December. Carrie's surgery and recovery from the broken ankle at one of the local hospitals was a difficult time. She suffered a lot of unnecessary pain. We vowed never to go

to that hospital again. When the hospital dismissed her, I was trying to finish the last field of corn. When she called for me to pick her up, I told her to wait just a little longer so I could finish. I paid for that mistake for a long time!"

I smiled at his comment and leaned forward. "But she didn't have the knee surgery, right?"

"Right. When we came home from the hospital, Carrie found it almost impossible to get out of the car. She couldn't manage crutches very well. I had to take her to work, put her in a wheelchair, and pick her up after work for almost two months. The whole situation made me angry. Not at Carrie. I just knew there had to be something causing this weakness. The orthopedic doctor was ready for her to have the knee replacement surgery. For some reason, I felt we needed a second opinion. I had always liked the surgeon who had done my shoulder surgery, so we made an appointment with him. At her visit to the new doctor, he said he would not do the surgery until he knew what was causing the weakness in her legs. With her quadriceps muscles so weak, she would not be able to do rehab. He recommended a neurosurgeon."

"You must have been very frustrated by this time. Carrie had pain in her knees, had trouble getting around, and no answers came your way." I peeked around the corner to see Carrie in the living room. "She is fast asleep."

"After her ankle healed, Carrie was able to drive herself back and forth to work and used a cane to get around easier in the house. She hated using it, thinking that people would suspect she was having trouble and ask questions. Her meeting with the neurosurgeon was terrifying. He had a horrible bedside manner. When he examined her weakened quadriceps, he couldn't believe she could still walk. He scheduled her for an EEG. This involved inserting needles into the muscles and then sending a current of electricity into them to see how they respond. She was tested in every muscle, even her tongue."

Jim sat back in his chair, envisioning the test. "That sounds awful! Was she in pain?"

"It must not have been too bad, because she didn't say much at the time. I picked her up from work a few days later to take her to get the results of the test. She hated to go because she was working on a major loan. This time the doctor's manner was a little more compassionate, but direct."

> *"I have to tell you what the test results tell me. I believe you have Amyotrophic lateral sclerosis or ALS, known as Lou Gehrig's disease. It could be something else but the only way to know for sure is to have a muscle biopsy. But I believe it is ALS."*

"I can still hear those words. We left the office and sat in the car for a few minutes. When I suggested we go home, she was still true to her work ethic."

> *"No, I have to go back to work to finish that loan."*

"I don't know if she knew exactly what ALS meant, as the doctor didn't try to explain it to her. He thought she should have the biopsy right away. I dropped Carrie off at the bank and cried as I drove home. I knew about the disease from my research, and it just couldn't be possible. I began reading everything I could about ALS, and something was telling me this was the wrong diagnosis. Carrie's conditions didn't exactly match the profile of these patients. The next day we had promised to go to Indiana to visit Jack. On the way we were able to decide together the diagnosis was wrong."

> *"Carrie, I've read everything I can get my hands on about ALS. From what the victims describe, that isn't what you are suffering. You do have the muscle weakness, but no cramps or twitching. You aren't having any trouble with your speech or with swallowing. And your hands and arms aren't affected."*
>
> *"So you think we might find out something else from the biopsy?"*
>
> *"I do, and I think we can't lose hope that you will find there is a better explanation."*
>
> *"That would be really great, because ALS is often painful and results in death."*

"Carrie's dad was very ill at this time and we nearly had to turn around and go back home because we feared he would not make it. We decided to go on and were able to tell Jack and his wife about her condition. Carrie never told her dad about her own problems, and he passed away not knowing anything about her condition."

"I remember when you called me to tell me there was a possibility of ALS, and you were very worried. You told me how much research you were doing, practically directing the doctors!" I smiled at my brother.

 56

"Inclusion body myositis. I had never heard of it. Evidently, there is limited knowledge about the disease. Whenever I type it into my computer, it redlines the word myositis. No, it is not a spelling error! This is what the muscle biopsy determined. Carrie went to the city for the first biopsy. There are three distinct features of muscle tissue, when stained with a red dye, that determine if a patient has ALS or IBM. Carrie's tissue revealed two features but ruled out ALS. We decided to get a second biopsy at the Mayo clinic in Minnesota, where we met with another neurosurgeon. The second biopsy found the third missing feature in Carrie's muscles, and it was her conclusion that she had Sporadic Inclusion Body Myositis. She could not determine the cause, when it started, or give Carrie any hope for a cure or medication to stop its progression. Some doctors argue that it is an autoimmune disorder where the white blood cells attack healthy muscle tissue leaving holes in the muscle cell causing the atrophy. Others argue it is a misfolding of protein in the muscle tissue. No one knows for sure.

"Why me?" asked Carrie.

"Bad luck," replied the neurosurgeon.

"Will any of my grandchildren have this?"
Carrie's first concern was for the children.

"This is not a genetic disorder." Not much empathy in his response.

"What can we do?"

"Prepare for this to get worse, it will progress. It will not affect the heart. Only voluntary muscles

> *are affected. Some people progress faster than others."*

"The doctor recommended Carrie start taking steroids to help with the inflammation, and told us of a drug used to fight tissue rejection in transplant patients. After reading all the side effects we thought the drugs could kill her before the IBM did."

I checked my watch. Time always slipped by so quickly. "I've never heard all these details before. Jim and I have a dinner tonight with some friends. I want to hear more about this, but we have to run. We'll be back later this evening, but don't wait up for us. Tell Carrie we didn't want to wake her."

Chapter 11

Changing the House

I slept fitfully that night, thinking of the disease and its effect on Carrie and Colin and their life together. Jim and I awoke, showered, and dressed to meet them downstairs for breakfast. We smelled the distinct aroma of bacon and of fresh brewed coffee.

"Good morning! How'd you sleep?" Colin was busy in the kitchen, frying bacon.

I ignored his question. "What can I do to help?" I asked, as I poured myself a cup of coffee. "Is Carrie in the shower?"

"She's working out on her bike, and said we should not wait for her this morning. I don't think she slept very well last night." He turned over the bacon, and then cracked some eggs into a bowl. "Scrambled eggs okay with you?"

"Sure, you just have to have some salsa for Jim." I took out some bread and plopped it into the toaster. "I'll do the toast. Butter in the fridge?"

"I got some out, over there on the counter."

Ian drove up the gravel driveway, parked his truck, and

walked into the house. "Hey, looks like I'm just in time!" He hugged me and shook hands with Jim. "I'm starved! Got enough for me, too?"

"I figured you would show up. I want to show you some of the plans I have for the basement in the lake house, anyway. Grab some coffee, and we'll have breakfast up in short order."

We gathered in the breakfast nook after filling plates with bacon, eggs, and toast. I smiled at Ian, thinking of him and his two little girls. "What do you have the girls and Shari up to today, Ian?" I spread some jelly on my toast.

"The girls have dance class today and they are planning to go shopping for new swim suits for summer. I figured Dad would have something here for me to do. We are working on some furniture for our bedroom."

"Such talent!" Jim drank some orange juice; he wasn't a coffee drinker. "So, Ian, did you have a long romance like your folks?"

"We did. Shari and I have been together since high school. The girls have been such a blessing to us. Shari is an amazing mom."

"What do you hear from the other boys? Dean is in California, right? Are you going to get out to see them sometime, Colin?" I pictured Carrie and her limitations.

Colin looked at Ian, then at me. "There is no way we would get her into an airplane, so our only way to go would be to drive. And it's a long way! In the meantime, we have Ian's girls and John's four little boys here. Dean's kids love to be here at the farm, and Ian's girls play with them when they are here. Dean has a new job now, so we don't know

how often they will be able to come this way. Maybe we will make it a family trip sometime."

"Do you have any of Mom's cinnamon rolls left from yesterday?" Ian asked, taking his plate back to the kitchen.

"I think in the refrigerator on the bottom shelf."

I smiled. "I don't know how you kept up with all those boys. They are all so tall with bottomless pits for stomachs." Everyone laughed.

"I'm very proud of all the boys. They and their wives are all a big help to Carrie. We get to babysit with either Ian's girls or a couple of John's boys fairly often, and Carrie looks forward to it. The girls are a little easier for her, and she can only have two of the boys at a time to watch. They keep you jumping! Usually at either Thanksgiving or Christmas we have Dean's kids along with the other six, and it is quite an affair." He rolled his eyes and sat back in his chair, obviously very proud of his family.

I remembered Carrie's dad and was curious about his illness and death. "Colin, didn't Carrie spend a lot of time caring for her dad?"

"Oh, yes, that was quite a difficult time for her. George was very demanding and expected Carrie to be available at his beck and call. He looked to me, too, in fact. His health became a real problem while he was living at the house, so we had to put him in the assisted living facility. Even there Carrie had to make trips to be with him and take care of business for him. She took her duty to him as a daughter very seriously."

"Was it easy to get things resolved after his passing? That would have added another responsibility for her as well, as Margaret couldn't handle the legalities."

"You're right. He had sold all of his farm machinery and finally sold the house to Ian and Shari. He had also ended any partnership with his brother. All in all, the estate was not as difficult as it might have been, partially because Carrie was so involved paying his bills and such when he was alive. Now she and Margaret share in some farm property. He was like Dad, in that he never bought large tracts of land for farming, just small acreage. So now Carrie charges me cash rent to farm the ground! Something wrong with that picture?" He shrugged his shoulders and threw up his arms.

I poured another cup of coffee. "You were telling us about the diagnosis when we talked yesterday. When did you start addressing her needs going forward?"

"Well, the first thing we did after the folks' death was to begin remodeling this kitchen and garage area. We had built the garage, but it wasn't connected to the house. There were steps up to the porch and the front entrance. With the help of Ian and Cal, who helps with the farming, we started drawing up plans as to how we might change the structure of the old house." Colin walked into his office and brought out the plans used for the remodel, spreading them out on the table. "It's kind of hard to imagine what the old kitchen looked like at this point."

"I remember it well, trust me. That tiny little kitchen would be impossible for Carrie to maneuver." I left my chair and peered over his shoulder at the design.

"We took out the north wall of the house, making a larger kitchen with an island, a huge bathroom and closet area, a laundry room, and an entrance was on ground level. We still have the porch, accessible from the sunroom on the

west side here. There is just one step down from the laundry room into the garage, so Carrie can manage that with her walker, but I've now made a ramp there. By connecting the house to the garage, we don't have to worry about her slipping on ice or snow. We spent a lot of time measuring for a wheel chair or electric scooter in the floor plan, so Carrie would be able to get around everything and through doorways. Carrie decided to retire from the bank before we were completely finished. The walking and worries about ice and snow in winter helped her make the decision."

"We added the patio in a little later. We built the porch and patio with a fire pit. Carrie can go out on the porch there and sit in a chair to enjoy the fire, or she can get down onto the patio as well with some assistance. The whole family has enjoyed that patio for all except the coldest days of winter."

"And now the kids have a play house as well," added Ian. "They all spend hours there when they are all together at Nana and Papa's house. Dad and my hired man Cal and I had fun building that structure, and it's where we can watch the kids from the patio."

"We couldn't let Jim get ahead of us, building one for your grandson!" Colin patted Jim on the back.

"You guys go do your thing, and I'll clean up. I'll be glad to fix something for Carrie when she gets to the kitchen." I gathered up the remaining plates to take to the sink and dishwasher. "Remember, I want to hear more about the progression of the disease at some point. I still can't remember the name!"

Chapter 12

Progression

The sun set to the west of the farm, leaving a brilliant red on the horizon. "Red sky in morning, sailor take warning!" said Colin, recalling a familiar phrase from our parents. The four of us sat around the dining room table, enjoying a slice of Carrie's delicious cherry pie.

"Carrie, this is so good," I noted. "You are the best pie maker I know."

"Thanks, Mary. These cherries have special memories for me. Marcie helped me pit these this year. It's getting a little harder for me to manage the pitting, so I appreciate all the help I can get. Colin found me this cherry pitter device." She lowered her chair slightly in line with the table, showed me her new gadget, and took a bite from her plate.

"Okay, so now I want to go back to where we left off last time on your search for answers about . . . what was the name of the disease again?" I looked to Carrie for her response.

"Inclusion Body Myositis, but you can probably better remember it as IBM. Then the Mayo clinic doctor added

'Sporadic' in front of it. That's not something you need to remember." Carrie smiled, teasing me about my memory.

Carrie recalled the next steps. "I began seeing a neurologist in the city. When he heard the diagnosis from Mayo, he told us he didn't recommend the steroid treatments. Nothing he had read showed any positive results and the side effects were worse. Colin and I made the decision not to use any of the drugs recommended. Our general doctor retired, so Colin encouraged me to see a doctor at a hospital not far from here, who had also been your mom's doctor and my dad's doctor. Even though he didn't know much about my condition, he has been studying up on it since we started going there."

Colin sat back in his chair and rubbed his chin. "I began to feel like I knew more about this condition than the doctors by now and knew we would have to be our own advocates to determine what we were going to do to make Carrie's life more tolerable. As I read more and more articles on IBM, I had to be careful what I shared with Carrie. Finally one day, she told me not to tell her anymore details." He stopped to place his arm around her shoulders, and then continued.

"We did start to go to a support group meeting. The Muscular Dystrophy Association sponsored the meeting. We met one man, Ken, who also had IBM and we both found him to be very helpful. Most of the other people in the group had ALS and we were both grateful to have met them. Almost all who started the group have passed on now or are incapable of coming to the meetings. Ken has had IBM for about five years longer than Carrie and is now completely limited to getting around in a power chair. He

can stand and transfer to a chair, but walks very little. Carrie thinks his progression is slower, and it hasn't affected his flexor muscles in his fingers as it has hers. Every patient is different."

"Have they made any progress on drugs more effective with IBM?" I stood and walked to the kitchen to get the coffee pot. Carrie pulled away from the table in her power chair, and turned toward the living room.

"If you will excuse me, I'll back out of this conversation and head for my recliner. I need to get my feet up."

With a fresh cup of coffee, Colin continued. "The only hope of any drug now is being evaluated in clinical trials. Bimagrumab developed by Novartis, has shown promise in stopping the progression and actually building muscle tissue. The trials began in 2013 and were supposed to finish by 2016. Carrie even tried to enroll in the trials, but doctors who worked to get patients enrolled had already booked the research facilities. She didn't have a doctor advocate, but it would have been hard to get her to Kansas City or Columbus for the testing. Recent developments have shown the drug has not increased the walking distance in patients, as we hoped. This was one of the primary outcomes measured in the test. While the clinical trials are still going on, this would be a setback for the release of the drug. It is an infused medication biological in composition. Because of the infusion, tests were to make sure the body doesn't reject it over time. As of April, 2016, the drug company announced the trials had a setback."

"So are you and Carrie holding out hope for this?" asked Jim, finishing his pie.

"Patients in the original trial are now all on the full

dosage to see if everything is going to be okay. I haven't told Carrie all of this. I'm just following her wishes to not tell her so much. Funny. She has always known I sometimes only tell her what she needs to know, or I tell her what I want her to hear. She worries a lot and I feel like it's my job to protect her so she doesn't worry. I guess I'm not doing a very good job though, as she still worries."

"I think she probably inherited that from her dad," I commented. "I remember how George used to worry all the time about the farming situation. Maybe the weather was too dry or too wet. Crop prices were too low, when the yield was high. The cost of farming was increasing. He was definitely a worrier."

"I heard those comments all the time he was alive. It was sometimes hard to stay positive, since we worked together on so many things. But I always had Dad to keep me positive. And I can definitely get on my knees and pray!" The three of us laughed as he expressed his attitude.

Jim handed me his plate and turned to Colin. "So tell us about the new plant near the edge of town."

Chapter 13

New Help for Carrie

C olin sipped coffee from his mug, contemplating where to start with the story of the plant. "2015 was a game changer. It actually started in 2013 when Illinois ventured into the medical marijuana age. Dean had a friend from Chicago who asked him if our family would have any ground to sell for development of a production facility. Ian also got involved and started promoting the idea at the local development council, where he was a member. One thing led to another and our town landed one of the facilities in the company planning. A farm Ian leased proved to be an ideal location as none of my farms would work for the project. Ian was able to convince the owner to sell ten acres, and the city worked the area into the TIF (Tax Increment Financing) district. In six months, the company built a twenty million dollar facility to grow and process medical cannabis. I was so proud of the boys, I could burst." He laughed and revealed a broad smile. Carrie returned to join them in the dining room.

"So how did that effect you and your issues, Carrie?"

"My IBM was on the list of conditions approved for medical cannabis. This was the boys' driving force. Then the developer asked Ian to be the general manager of the facility. In 2016, I enrolled in the medical cannabis program. After a long process of getting a doctor to fill out the necessary application and both of us fingerprinted, I was ready to start using marijuana. I would never try it in high school, but forty-three years later, my sons convinced me to give it a try."

The three of them laughed at Carrie's statement. "So this all took place after you found the lake house, Colin?"

Colin's face lit up with excitement. "Oh, yes, but not entirely. One day over dinner in 2015, Ian told us about a house at Lake of the Ozarks coming up for sale, and he would have first chance at it. We all discussed our love of the lake and decided we would take a weekend to see the house. This could be our vacation home. So Ian, Shari and the girls, and us, all took a trip to the Ozarks. Ian got the key to the house so we could see how it might work out for Carrie." Colin stood up, stretching his back in the process. He walked into the kitchen and retrieved a glass from the cabinet, filling it with water from the refrigerator door. "Can I get anyone a glass of water?

"None for me, thanks. As I remember, the house wasn't handicapped accessible?" I turned to watch him walk back to the table, noting how much he resembled our dad.

"Right, Mary. The rooms were small and the driveway and yard weren't the best for us either. We decided while we were there to wander around to see what else might be available. Shari got on the Internet and found a resort area with townhouses for sale. They looked inviting, so

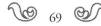

we made an appointment to see one recently completed. We fell in love with it. Especially Carrie, as she could see the opportunity for us to get away from the farm, spend time together, and have a special place for the kids and grandkids to enjoy. We took down all the information about the townhouse and later returned home." He took a long drink from his glass.

Carrie continued. "When we got home, we talked at length about the positives, including how Colin might be able to make it more accessible. Ian and Shari were very much for the idea, and offered to help pay for a pontoon boat, as a slip for a boat was part of the real estate purchase. It would be a big investment for us, and we didn't want to obtain yet another loan on the property. You remember Colin talking about my ESOP plan and how much it had accumulated?"

"Yes, but there are consequences for early withdrawals from those accounts," said Jim.

"You are right about that. But, we talked to our investment broker and our tax people. Weighing the options, we decided to take the money we needed out of the ESOP, pay the taxes, and set aside money we were going to need for furnishings, window coverings, as well as the boat and the lift. We wanted that property, and I bought it with my company savings plan!" Carrie was proud of their decision.

"It is such a special place, and I know the kids love going there. You have both told me how much you enjoy being there with just the two of you. I understand the golf cart gets you all over the subdivision and adds interesting aspects to your days there. Didn't you build a lot of the furniture for the house, Colin?"

"That is still part of the process. When we have some extra time here at the farm, I'm often in the shop putting together a side table, a coffee table, or some other extra piece for the house. It's amazing how much has been added since we bought it. Now we are working on the basement. Part of it is already finished, but we want to add space for the grandkids' playroom under the front half. One of the great things about the layout is the porches and railings at both the upstairs and downstairs. We don't have to worry about the kids getting out and falling, so it is a pretty safe place for all of them to be. Right now they are sleeping in pup tents and sleeping bags on the basement carpet."

"Tell us about the boat dock and the boat." I smiled at Colin's enthusiasm about the lake house.

"Carrie loves the boat, but you can imagine how hard it would be to get her into and out of the boat. The lift company installed the lift that first spring after we bought the house, and the boat was next. There is a walkway from the sidewalk on the shore out to the covered boat dock, but it is not stable enough for Carrie to navigate. It is very easy for her to be out of balance, and then she is afraid of falling. Cal and I acquired some heavy metal and designed a ramp. With hinges, it folds in the middle for storage, but lays flat across that step from the shore to the walkway. Carrie can maneuver her power chair onto the ramp and then onto the walkway all the way to the dock."

"Colin has to be right there with me, as I'm pretty nervous about going down the ramp." Carrie smiled and shifted in her chair.

"The next challenge was getting her from the dock into the boat. With the lift, we can raise the floor of the boat to

the same level as the dock. Cal and I bolted on another ramp with hinges to fold out onto the dock from the boat. Carrie can drive her power chair right into the boat and back it into a space right behind the driver seat. It works really well, and she loves those boat rides." Colin had been sketching out the ramps to demonstrate them to Jim and me.

"You have done so much to help Carrie with her limitations. I'm not sure where you got all that talent, although our dad and older brother are very industrious folks." I winked at Colin and reached out for Jim's hand. "Even Jim has picked up some carpentry skills, but he will probably stick with his gardening."

"When Carrie tells me of a particular difficulty and what might be better for her, my brain starts working on how I might make it happen. There are many things I can create and build. I just can't make the disease go away." A tear formed in the corner of his eye and trickled down his cheek, and his words caught in his throat as he reached over to hold Carrie's hand.

Chapter 14

Carrie's Perspective

Later in the afternoon, Carrie and I had some time together preparing food for the four of them to cook out. I observed Carrie as she moved around her kitchen. Using her power chair, she was able to reach most things in the cabinets and move things from the island to the sink or to the stove. Occasionally, she used the built-in lift to raise the height of the chair.

"Tell me about the grandkids. Are you able to keep up with them?" I wondered.

"The girls are very easy. They like to help me, and like to do some of the things that are easier for me. The boys are so busy! Colin has to help me out when they come. If I just have the older two boys, they stay occupied in the playroom with toys. And I love having all of them around."

"What do you want me to get out for the salad?"

"There are carrots in the vegetable drawer. We will have to peel and cut them, as I like the regular carrots better than those little ones in the packages. They have more flavor. I usually dice them for the salad."

I found the carrots and the peeler and took them to the sink. "It must be hard for you to handle this peeler, isn't it?"

"I can handle it. It just takes me a while, but I have lots of time to spend in the kitchen. I sometimes fix lunch for Colin when he and Cal are here. Either Colin comes home to get something to eat or they go out for lunch when he is in the fields. It is a lonely time for me when they are planting or harvesting. Colin leaves early in the morning, and he sometimes doesn't get home until eight or nine o'clock. I like to have him here when I take a shower in the morning. The shower is set up great for me, but I'm always afraid I'll fall." Carrie moved her chair near the island.

"Do you wait for him to be here to shower?" I stopped peeling and turned to Carrie.

"Usually. At Thanksgiving last year when the kids were all here and we were cooking a big dinner, I fell. When I fall, my knees buckle and I fall backwards with my legs under me. In addition to hitting my head on the floor, I couldn't get up. I couldn't even roll over because my legs were splayed out beside me. Luckily, Colin was right here in the kitchen to help me. I had bruises on my knees and a bump on my head. It was the worst fall I've had. It just happens without warning, and I didn't have time to grab for support. That's why now I have this call button. Colin insisted we get it in case he isn't right here with me and my phone isn't within reach."

I could see the fear in Carrie's face as she related her story. In an article I read, there were references to balance in the IBM diagnosis. Plus, I knew Carrie had pain in her knees, because the pain was the reason she first went to a doctor for possible surgery. I turned back to the sink and the carrots. "Does your sister Margaret ever come out to help you or to just spend time with you?"

"Margaret comes to the farm when we invite her for a family get together. She has her own friends, and now she has moved to a high rise in the city, so she is farther away. I don't want to ask her for help, mainly because I don't know what I would have her do for me." She stood up with her walker and maneuvered around to the refrigerator. "Would you like some iced tea?"

"I'll get that." I took the tea pitcher out of the refrigerator and set it on the counter, then retrieved two glasses from the cabinet. "Let's take a break. Need sugar?"

"No, I don't like my tea sweet." She paused. "You know I have a prescription for cannabis for my pain."

"Yes, Colin told us. How did you know what to get? I have no clue as to how that is handled through the pharmacies."

"Ian has been a big help in teaching us the various kinds of products available. What I use is inhaled through one of those vapor tubes used by people who are trying to quit smoking. It is specifically for the pain, and it does help me. I keep it in a drawer where the kids won't find it, and I go into the bathroom to use it if they are here. For so long I was concerned about what people were thinking when they saw me using a walker or a cane, so now I have to be cautious about my grandchildren seeing me smoking my pot!" Carrie laughed at her dilemma. "I had to get a specific doctor to help me with the prescription. My regular doctor doesn't want to prescribe it."

"I'm sure he must know it helps you now, though. He seems to be really concerned for your welfare." I carried

our glasses to the island and sat on a stool. "You do have a housekeeper to help you, right?"

"Oh, yes. She comes every week and does everything I ask of her. I haven't been upstairs for a long time, so I hope it's looking okay."

"It looks fabulous, and it's so comfortable. Your bedroom downstairs was first my folks' bedroom, then converted to a family room, now back to a bedroom. The bathroom in the hallway is so small it would be impossible for you to get around. It's a good thing Colin added that big one on the other side of the kitchen." I emptied a packet of sweetener into my tea and stirred it pensively. "I remember when my mom had a housekeeper when she was working. She would pull out the couch and chairs from the wall to make sure the housekeeper vacuumed behind them. So funny!"

"I do try to make sure Lexi covers everything, as I've always been particular with my home. She runs the vacuum and mops the bathroom floors. But Colin insists on cleaning these wood floors. He is afraid someone might ruin them with water or cleaners."

"You know, if you get lonely when Colin is in the fields, you can always call someone to come over for tea or coffee." I thought back to Carrie's comment about Colin in the fields.

"I have a special neighbor who stops by and calls me. And I go out with some other girls for lunch once a month. That gives me something to look forward to. This month I managed to get the chair onto the back of the car and drove it to meet them for lunch. When we left, we had a little trouble getting it lined up again for the lift on the car,

so that was a little embarrassing. Everyone in the parking lot was trying to help, and I couldn't do much except give instructions. When something like that happens, it makes me afraid to go out by myself again."

They sat in silence for a few moments, considering Carrie's comment. "What challenges do you have now, Carrie?" I asked.

"I'm losing the ability to make a fist in both hands, especially the right. I can use my thumb still against my fingers, but can't bend my fingers to grasp anything. I just have to take my time to make sure I have a good grip before trying to lift or carry anything. Lately, I have also had a little trouble swallowing my food. It takes me forever to eat because of that. Then again, I don't eat so much, so that's a good thing!" She laughed to put me at ease. "I'm going to go out to the golf cart and take Max for a run."

"I noticed you have him on a chain all the time. You have told me stories of him running all the way into town if he gets loose. How do you handle him on the cart?"

"Oh, we have gotten calls to pick up Max so many times. But he loves to get on the golf cart with me. I take him out to the wind tower and the alfalfa fields and let him run for a while. I just sit and wait for him, then call him back. He comes back pretty quickly and jumps back onto the cart with me."

"Well, I'm going to get back to my carrots, or we won't have them ready for the salad for supper. Jim is probably having a great time with Colin out and about." I took my glass back to the sink and returned to my assignment.

Chapter 15

The Lake House

Late that summer, Jim and I were passing through Missouri and Lake of the Ozarks. We stopped to spend a couple of days with Colin and Carrie at the new lake house. Carrie and Colin, Jim and I, all gathered on the back porch with a view of the golf course through the trees.

"Did everyone get a good night's sleep?" asked Colin.

"I slept well, but I have such vivid dreams. In these dreams, I'm always healthy and able to run and exercise. I'm never disabled. I guess they help me face each new day." Carrie smiled, taking her coffee cup between both hands to sip Colin's vanilla and cinnamon coffee blend.

"How interesting, Carrie. It's kind of like your mind doesn't want to recognize your limitations. I think that is really cool." I rested my hand on Carrie's arm. "Look! There goes a deer across the golf course."

Colin laughed. "We see them all the time here. There will be some more homes built behind us here, so we won't have as good a view then. But we always have the boat and the lake. Anyone up for a boat ride later?"

"Absolutely," said Jim and I at the same time. Jim took a drink from his diet soda.

"We have a favorite restaurant for breakfast, so when everyone is ready we will take a drive there to eat before our boat ride." Colin stood up from the table and carried his cup into the kitchen. On his cue, everyone followed to get dressed.

The restaurant reminded me of a cafe in our hometown, serving the locals with the country fare of egg plates, pancakes, and waffles. The tables were not crowded together, allowing plenty of room for Carrie's power chair to pass between them. Colin removed a chair from the table for Carrie's place, and she pulled into the spot and adjusted the height of her chair. Orders came quickly to the table and I observed Carrie eating.

"Carrie, you seem to be swallowing a little better than the last time we were with you. Are you doing better?"

"While we were getting dressed to come here, I took a few puffs of the pipe. It seems to relax the muscles in my throat to allow me to swallow better. It doesn't take me so long to eat now." Carrie smiled, pleased with the results of the cannabis.

"That's a miracle in itself. I was really concerned when we saw you struggling with swallowing."

The food disappeared quickly from the plates, and Jim insisted on paying the tab. "And I plan to put some gas in that boat, too, Colin."

The process Colin had described about getting Carrie into the boat for the boat ride was a little cumbersome, but really worked efficiently. Within a few minutes of arriving at the dock, the chair was downloaded, the ramp in place

to transfer to the dock, and the second ramp onto the deck folded for Carrie's transfer. With Carrie between the benches on the boat, Colin lowered the boat back down into the water, climbed into the pilot seat, and we were on our way.

I wore a white cap, but Carrie allowed the wind to blow through her hair. The joy she felt with the boat and the lake were obvious in her smile. Even Jim was enjoying the ride, with his life jacket in place. Not a swimmer, he took no chances. Colin pointed out special points of interest along the shore, including some favorite eating spots and other areas they considered for a home purchase. They gassed up the boat at one of the dock facilities, and finally returned after almost two hours on the water. Their faces were pink from the sun, despite the sunscreen.

"Mary, I love your hat. Does it stay on pretty well? I need to get me one." Carrie asked as they made their way back to the car.

"I'll just give you this one. You can keep it here for the boat. I have another one back home I can use."

"Thank you so much."

After some rest, we went to the clubhouse for dinner and enjoyed a delightful meal. "We come here often," said Colin. "It's pretty convenient for us, and we can usually bring the golf cart here instead of the car. Then we go for a drive around the complex to enjoy the views of the golf course and the houses."

"Mary, let's go for a cart ride when we get back. You can drive, and I'll navigate." Carrie was eager to show me around the area.

I took the driver seat with Carrie beside me. We drove

on the roads to see all the houses, then got on the golf cart trail, since it was after hours, and took a tour of the golf course. Carrie pointed out new houses under construction, areas for new houses, and all the features of the golf course. For one hour, we were just sisters, enjoying each other, with no mind to the limitations Carrie would again face on their return to the house.

"We just need to plug in the cart there at the outlet," said Carrie as she reached for her walker to climb out of the cart. "And Colin says to make sure the key is turned off."

"This was fun, Carrie. Thanks so much for the tour."

We maneuvered up the wooden ramp Colin constructed to the back door, closed the garage door, and went inside the house.

Colin was reading from his computer screen. "Hey, Carrie. There is a new drug in research called Arimoclomal. Seems there is a lot of anticipation for the results."

I smiled. Abiding love. Never give up hope. Always offer support. Love beyond measure.

Chapter 16

Freedom for Carrie

Fall and winter were busy times for Colin and Carrie. They celebrated an early Christmas with Dean and his family at the farm, spending part of the holidays at the lake house with Ian and John and their families. Colin and Carrie were also able to spend time at the lake, usually a weeklong restful time for both of them. Colin began work on the additional room in the basement with the help of Ian when he and Shari could get away for a weekend with the girls in tow. Carrie and I kept up with family news by phone. In early March, I called her for an update.

"Hi, Carrie. Colin tells me you have a new van." Colin had mentioned the van to me, noting it would give Carrie more freedom, a new independence.

"Yes, it is amazing."

"I don't quite understand how it works for your chair, so I hoped you could describe it to me." When Colin told me about an extending ramp, I couldn't picture it.

"There is a ramp that automatically comes out of the passenger side door of the van. Then the van kneels to

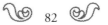

lower the floor of the van so the ramp isn't so steep. It's not like you would picture any other van, as the floor is much lower than a regular floor."

"That helps me picture it better. So you can just drive the chair up the ramp and into the van, then turn it to the driver position?"

"That's right. There is a locking mechanism to make sure the chair doesn't move once it's in place. Actually, there are three of these locking positions. One is the driver, one the passenger, and one is sort of in the middle of the van to ride as a passenger. I can move from that middle position to a bench behind it to ride with Max if we are on a longer trip to the lake. All the chairs are leather and are set up for easy removal. Colin can take out either the driver seat or the passenger seat to make room for my chair. Once I have the chair in place, I can raise it to the right height."

"Have you been driving it? Is it pretty easy to manage?" I was still having trouble visualizing the van and her access.

"I'm doing better all the time. The break and the accelerator button are one control, so I really have to concentrate on what I'm doing. When we drive down to the lake, Colin is always drawing or thinking about something, so he doesn't talk much. I always want him to do more talking. Now I told him it will be okay to be quiet, so I can concentrate on driving." Carrie laughed.

"Now you will be able to get out on your own without Colin while he is in the field?" I was elated at Carrie's new freedom.

"Yes. You remember me saying I couldn't get into the restaurant here in town where the kids always go? Well, Ian talked to the owner about how I couldn't get up the steps

to the front door. He told Ian to have me come through the kitchen in the back, and we had never even thought of that. We went there last Friday night for dinner, and I was so excited to be able to go. The food was wonderful, and the owner told me to just let him know when we wanted to come in, and he would make sure the back door was accessible."

"And there was no problem with coming in through the kitchen?"

"No. He said they sometimes have people tour the kitchen, as they are very proud of how clean it is. It really is neat, clean and tidy. I'm thinking the girls I go to lunch with can now go there. Two of us are in wheelchairs or motorized chairs, so that is always a limitation with some restaurants."

I could hear the joy in Carrie's voice as she related her new freedoms. "That is awesome, Carrie. How is everything else going?"

"I've been cleaning out some lower cabinets in the kitchen. I can reach these from my chair without getting down on the floor, and I have my grabber stick to wipe down the shelves. Some of the pots and pans are too heavy for me, so I seldom use them. I've decided to take those to the lake house. Colin is always there with me to help get them to the stove or sink. He wants to go there for this next week before planting season to work on the basement. It takes me quite a while to get everything together before we go." "That sounds like a great idea, Carrie. Is he working on anything else for you at the moment?"

"It's funny you ask that. He mentioned the other day he needed to work on some things to make my days a little

easier where he sees me struggling, but I told him not to do so much. Every time I give up something I'm struggling to do, I never get it back. I need to keep trying to keep up my strength to some extent. But he did find a high toilet seat for our bathroom, which has been a big help. We found out recently a man we know who has ALS is now in a nursing home. It reminds me how lucky I am to have IBM rather than ALS. I need to keep doing all I can to slow down the progression of the disease." Carrie cleared her throat to control her emotions.

"Is Colin getting ready for planting?"

"Not yet. The doctor sent him for an MRI, and he has some issue in his back affecting one of his legs. The muscle in his right leg is weak, so they are thinking some nerve damage. He has another appointment with our doctor this week, so we'll see what he says. He was wondering what we would do if he has to have a procedure. He has planting to do, and he knows I need him quite a bit. I told him we have two sons to help if we need them. We can figure it out."

"And you have a sister and brother-in-law who can lock up our house in Texas and be there to help you. Just give us a call!" Carrie and I both laughed. "Seriously, Carrie, that's what you two are all about. You always find a way to work through everything together."

Carrie was quiet for a moment. "Thank you. I love you."

"Love you back. Talk to you soon." I clicked off the call in time to see Jim coming home for lunch after running some errands. I told him about Colin's back, and described the van as Carrie had described it to me. We also pulled up pictures of side-entry vans on the Internet, some of which also included interior pictures.

"I'm not sure how good I'd be at running the newfangled equipment Colin has there on the farm. But I could learn." Jim echoed my idea of going to help.

When Colin called to visit with me the next time, he said the issue with his leg didn't require immediate surgery and he wasn't in any pain. At least for the moment, that sidetrack was off their minds, probably until after harvest. He also told me he was doing more and more of the cooking in the kitchen and could see he was going to have to be more available for Carrie in the future.

I cried when I hung up the phone. So unfair. Such a beautiful couple and faced with so many challenges in their young life. Colin would soon be sixty-three, Carrie just sixty-two. Those images of travel and adventures in the future when they were young are now restricted to spending time at the lake with family. Despite the challenges, they are happy being together and working together to find joy in each day. The boys and their families share adventures and joys in their lives. Soon there will be joy in two more grandchildren. There is no long-term plan for the future, only a decision as to how long Colin can continue to participate in the farming. His first priority is and always will be for Carrie and their abiding love.

Acknowledgements

I am always grateful to my wonderful husband, Jerry, for his patience with me and his support in working to get my writing published. He has spent many hours looking at me from the back, as I focus on the computer in front of me. In addition, a special thanks to my family and friends who have read the story and helped with some ideas: Jerry; my daughter Heidi; my sweet sister-in-law Judy and brother Dave; and Pastor Bobby Vitek for his sermon on abiding love. A special thank you to WOW (Women of Words), my writer's group in Fredericksburg, Texas. You have all contributed to making my story ready for publication. Janie Goltz, my editor and friend, your review was such a great benefit to those who will read these words.

About the Author

Linda Kay Christensen, a former farm girl from the central Illinois town of Delavan, has enjoyed many years as a bank manager, a self-employed accountant and tax preparer (CPA), and an online instructor for Keller Graduate School (DeVry University). She earned her bachelor's in Business Management and her Masters in Human Resources from the University of Illinois, Springfield. Linda's history of writing has included everything from business communication, teaching, and journaling, to occasional poetry and writing a daily blog. Her inspiration for WE PROMISED is based on a true story. This is the fourth book in the series of the five stages of love as depicted in five prints by C. Clyde Squires, given to her grandmother in 1916 as a wedding gift. The people the artist has created in these prints will come alive in Linda's series of the "five stages of love." Life in the time of these prints has changed dramatically, allowing for a new look at the stories behind a modern view of the prints.

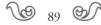

Linda helped her mother, Wilma Diekhoff, complete her memoirs in a book that includes 200 recipes from family and friends. Wilma held a book signing at Barnes and Noble at the age of 82. "Flavors from the Past: Memoirs and Recipes of Wilma Weiland Diekhoff" is only available in digital format with various ebook publishers. Linda's first romance fiction novel was published in August of 2014. "Annie's Love" addresses mother love in its various interpretations. It is available in digital and print. "Sophie Writes a Love Story", also available in digital and print, is based on puppy love, the second stage of love in the prints. The third in the series is "Out of Darkness to Accepted Love", published in early 2016. A short story "Antics" was published in 2016 in the Creative Writing Institute's Explain!, a themed anthology.

Linda is married to Jerry, a former engineer now retired and a master gardener. They live in Fredericksburg, Texas. Many of the characters who contribute to Linda's writings are the result of extensive travel. She is a member of the Writers' League of Texas in Austin and Women of Words in Fredericksburg.

Follow me at: http://senioradventureswithlindakay.blogspot.com

Printed in the United States
By Bookmasters